Parent's Introduction

We Both Read Books are delightful stories which **both** a parent **and** a child can participate in reading aloud. Developed in conjunction with early reading specialists, the books invite parents to read the more sophisticated text on the left-hand pages, while children are encouraged to read the right-hand pages, which have been specially written for beginning readers. The parent's text is preceded by a "talking parent" icon: ☺ ; the children's text is preceded by a "talking child" icon: ☺ .

Educators know that nothing helps children learn to read more than by reading aloud with their parents. However, the concentration necessary for reading is often difficult for young children. That is why *We Both Read Books* offer short periods of reading by the child, alternating with periods of being read to by their parent. The result is a much more enjoyable and enriching experience for both!

Most of the words used in the child's text should be familiar to them. Others can easily be sounded out. An occasional difficult word will often be first introduced in the parent's text, distinguished with **bold lettering**. Pointing out these words, as you read them, will help familiarize them to your child. You may also find it helpful to read the entire book to your child the first time, then invite them to participate on the second reading.

We hope that both you and your children enjoy the *We Both Read Books* and that they will help start your children off on a lifetime of reading enjoyment!

We Both Read: The Emperor's New Clothes

———————————————————

We Both Read™ is a trademark of Treasure Bay, Inc.

Published by Treasure Bay, Inc.
50 Horgan Ave., Suite 12
Redwood City, CA 94061 USA

PRINTED IN SINGAPORE

Library of Congress Catalog Card Number: 97-62026
ISBN 1-891327-03-8

FIRST EDITION

We Both Read™ Books
Patent Pending

THE
EMPEROR'S
NEW CLOTHES

Adapted by Sindy McKay

from the story by Hans Christian Andersen

Illustrated by Toni Goffe

TREASURE BAY

Once upon a time there lived an emperor.
He was a rich emperor. He was a handsome emperor.
But most of all, he was a well-dressed emperor.

The emperor often paraded through town, showing off his **fine** and fancy clothes.

He would wave to the townspeople and say;

"I like fine new pants.

I like them. I do.

I like fine new hats,

and new socks and new shoes!"

One day the emperor met two strangers who claimed to be weavers of the very finest cloth.

"We make cloth more beautiful than any you can imagine!" said the first. "With a magical quality," said the second with a wink. "For some people have found they **cannot** even see it!"

The emperor replied;

"Some cannot see it?
Now how can that be?
Who cannot see it?
I hope it's not me."

The weavers assured him he would indeed be able to see it. For the fabulous cloth they made was invisible only to a fool.

This gave the emperor a wonderful idea! He could use this magical cloth to discover who in his town was a **fool**!

So he said to the weavers;

"You will make it for me.
I must see what you do.
I will give you my gold.
You will show me a fool."

The emperor gave the weavers chests of gold and provided them with weaving threads of the finest silk and silver. Then he sent them off to make their magic cloth while he waited impatiently.

And as he waited, the emperor thought about the magic cloth;

"I want to go see it.
I have to! I do!
But if I *don't* see it,
then am *I* a fool?"

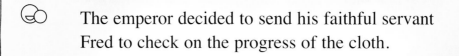

The emperor decided to send his faithful servant Fred to check on the progress of the cloth.

Fred went to the weaving loom where the weavers told him threads of silk and silver could be seen being woven into beautiful cloth.

Fred, however, saw nothing at all.

And Fred thought;

"I do not see it.

Not a thing do I see!

But I will not say so.

No fool will *I* be!"

Fred rushed back and told the emperor of the wondrous beauty of the cloth.

Excited by the news, the emperor gave the weavers more gold and expensive weaving thread. Then he sent them back to work on the cloth while he waited impatiently.

And as he waited, he thought;

 "I have to go see it!

I want to! Like Fred!

I don't think I'm a fool.

But first — I'll send Ted."

So Ted, another faithful servant, was sent to check on the progress of the cloth.

Ted went to the weaving loom where the weavers told him he could see that the cloth was now almost completed.

Ted, however, saw **nothing** at all.

And Ted thought;

"I do not see it.
There is nothing to see!
But I will not say so.
No fool will *I* be!"

Ted hurried back and told the emperor of the marvelous splendor of the cloth.

So excited was the emperor that he gave the weavers even **more** gold and expensive weaving threads! And the weavers were happy to take it all.

In fact, they were ecstatic!

Then the emperor said;

"It is time for a look.
It's a thing I must do!
And I know I will see it
for I am no fool."

The emperor, along with four more faithful servants, set out to see the cloth.

Together they went to the weaving loom where the weavers told them they could see the finished cloth in all its magnificent glory.

The emperor and his servants, however, saw nothing at all.

And each one thought;

"I do not see it.

Not a thing do I see!

But I will not say so.

No fool will *I* be!"

Each trusted servant extravagantly praised the beauty of the **cloth** he did not see.

"Brilliant!"

      "Amazing!"

           "Dazzling!"

                  "Indescribable!"

And the emperor enthusiastically agreed with their descriptions.

Then he turned to the weavers and said;

"I do love this cloth!
Now here's what you must do.
You must make me some pants
and a brand new coat, too."

So the weavers began making the emperor a very special **outfit**. Taking the "magic cloth" from the loom, they pretended to cut it out in the air with a huge pair of scissors, then stitched away at it with needles that held no thread.

Then they said to the emperor;

"Come now and see it!
The outfit is done!
No other is like it!
There is only one!"

The emperor rushed to see the weavers holding up their empty arms, as if displaying the emperor's new clothes. They bragged about the elegant pants and gushed over the long, flowing cape.

And the emperor exclaimed;

"Oh look! There it is!

My new outfit is done!

I love it so much!

Now I must try it on!

The weavers pretended to dress the emperor in his fine new outfit. As they placed the invisible cape on his shoulders, they marveled that it was "as light as a feather."

So light that one might think he had nothing on at all.

And the emperor declared;

⊙ "I *love* how it feels —
   like nothing at all!
   Look how it fits!
   It makes me look tall!"

Then the emperor turned to his trusted servants and asked what **they** thought of the **color** and fit.

Since none of these men were fools, none could admit they saw nothing at all.

So one at a time they remarked;

"It looks very cool."

"The color is right."

"It looks easy to wash."

"And the pants are not tight."

The next day the emperor proudly paraded through town, eager to show off his fine and fancy new clothes.

As he strutted down the street, a huge **crowd** began to gather.

And the emperor crowed;

"Just look at the crowd!
They love what they see!
It is not every day
they see so much of me!"

Never before had so many people come out to see the emperor's new clothes!

And, since no one in town wanted to be thought a fool, no one would admit there were no clothes to be seen.

So instead they all said;

"It looks good on him."

"It's not something *I'd* wear."

"How would you fix it
   if it got a tear?"

Then, at last, a tiny voice spoke up from the crowd.
The voice of a child.
The voice of the truth.

And the voice said;

"There is nothing to fix.
There is nothing to tear.
There is nothing to see
because nothing is there."

The townspeople could hardly believe their ears.
What was wrong with the child? Was he suggesting
that the emperor was **naked**?

And still the voice continued;

"He tells you it's there
but maybe he lies.
He looks naked to me.
And I have good eyes."

Then another small voice spoke up, agreeing with the **child**. Then another. And another.

The small voices swelled. Big voices joined in. Until finally the whole town knew.

The emperor was wearing no clothes.

And the voices said;

"He has nothing on."

"I see nothing! Do you?

"I see nothing on him."

"What the child says is true."

Soon everyone was seeing what was really there.
And what was really not.

As the laughter of the crowd filled the air,
the emperor marched on, insisting that the whole town must
be made up of fools.

But in his heart, the emperor knew who the **town** fool
really was.

And to himself he said;

"I know it is true
At last I can see.
I have found the town fool.
And the town fool is — *me*."

⮞ *The End* ⮜

**If you liked
The Emperor's New Clothes,
here are two other We Both Read™ Books
you are sure to enjoy!**

In this humorous and charming tale, a princess loses her golden ball and then makes promises to the frog who gets it back for her. But the princess does not want to keep her promises! To her surprise the frog appears at the castle door looking for the princess and all that she promised!